# Ark in the Park

# Ark in the Park

by Wendy Orr

illustrated by Kerry Millard

Henry Holt and Company

New York

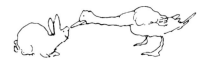

Henry Holt and Company, LLC, *Publishers since 1866*
115 West 18th Street, New York, New York 10011
Henry Holt is a registered trademark of Henry Holt and Company, LLC

First published in the United States in 2000 by Henry Holt and Company, LLC
Published in Canada by Fitzhenry & Whiteside Ltd.,
195 Allstate Parkway, Markham, Ontario L3R 4T8.
Originally published in Australia by HarperCollins Publishers, Australia.

Library of Congress Cataloging-in-Publication Data
Orr, Wendy.
Ark in the park / Wendy Orr; illustrated by Kerry Millard.
p. cm.
Summary: When her parents take her to visit a very special pet store
in the park across from her apartment, both Sophie and Mr. and
Mrs. Noah, the pet store owners, have their secret wishes fulfilled.
[1. Pet shops—Fiction. 2. Grandparents—Fiction.
3. Wishes—Fiction.] I. Millard, Kerry, ill. II. Title.
PZ7.0746Ar 2000 [Fic]—dc21 99-33342

ISBN 0-8050-6221-1 (hardcover)
1 3 5 7 9 10 8 6 4 2
ISBN 0-8050-6818-X (paperback)
1 3 5 7 9 10 8 6 4 2

First American hardcover and paperback editions
published in 2000 by Henry Holt and Company
Printed in Mexico

*To the memory of
Monsieur and Mémère Gunther
—W. O.*

*For Mum, for Jo and Phil
—K. M.*

# Ark in the Park

# Chapter 1

It was the biggest, the strangest, the most wonderful pet shop in the whole world.

"After all," said Mrs. Noah, "with a name like ours, what other kind of shop could we have?"

"And after all," said Mr. Noah, "with a name like ours, how else could we build it?"

So they built it like a ship, and they called it *The Noahs' Ark.*

It filled two whole blocks of the city they lived in and, instead of rocking on the deep blue sea, it sat in the middle of a wide, green park.

It had tall sails made of white glass. Birds nested high up in the masts, and sang and swooped back and forth and up and down inside the sails.

It had seven different levels, so that animals who didn't like each other didn't have to see each other.

There were ponies and lambs and cats and dogs and rabbits and turtles and every other kind of pet in the world.

"We wanted to have lions and elephants," said Mrs. Noah, "but they're not really *practical* pets."

"Not very safe for children," said Mr. Noah, and they were both sad for a moment because they didn't have any children.

"Of course," said Mr. Noah, "if we had children they'd be grown up by now."

"Then we'd have grandchildren," said Mrs. Noah.

"We have everything else we've ever wished for," Mr. Noah said. "Some things are just not possible."

But every night, Mr. and Mrs. Noah wished one impossible wish—they wished that they had grandchildren.

# Chapter 2

The city where Mr. and Mrs. Noah lived was a very big, very busy city. All around the ark, as far as you could see, were tall, tall buildings.

One of the very tallest was an apartment building. And in an apartment at the very cloud-scraping top lived Sophie.

At the bottom of the building was a road, but it was a very long way down. And on the other side of the road was the park, but Sophie was not allowed to go there alone. Her mother said she was too young to cross the road, and her father said that the park was too dangerous.

"It's so big, you could get lost," he said. "And you wouldn't know anyone who could help you."

But her mother was always busy with the twins, and her father was always busy at work, so they hardly ever had time to take her.

The people in the apartments near Sophie and her family went out to work all day and did not have children. There were girls around her age who lived on the second floor, but they visited their grandparents or their cousins in the country every weekend.

Sophie's mother and father came from a country a long way away, and Sophie did not have grandparents or aunts and uncles to visit. She did not have cousins to call on the phone or visit on holidays.

At school she tried not to hear when the other children talked about going to the zoo with their grandparents, or picnics and pillow fights with their cousins.

When she was not at school, Sophie spent most of
her time looking out the window and wishing.

She watched people walking in the park and children playing. She watched them picking grass for their
guinea pigs, playing ball with their dogs, and riding
their ponies.

Most of all, she watched *The Noahs' Ark.*

From her window the great glass sails looked like real sails filled with wind and, if she half closed her eyes and rocked on her seat, she could imagine that it really was a ship at sea.

"What *are* you watching, Sophie?" her mother would ask.

"Nothing," Sophie always answered.

Every night Sophie made two impossible wishes.

She wished for a pet and she wished for cousins. But then she made a third wish that was not quite impossible. Sophie wished she could visit *The Noahs' Ark.*

# Chapter 3

In three more days it would be Sophie's birthday—her seventh birthday.

Sophie liked the sound of seven. It was a strong number, a magic number. It was the kind of number that wishes could come true on.

"No party," said her mother, "not with the twins so small. But you can ask a friend for tea."

Sophie asked Ann-Marie. Ann-Marie was her best friend at school. She asked her to come for tea on Saturday afternoon.

Sophie woke up very early on Saturday morning. She washed and dressed, cleaned her teeth and brushed her hair, and still the sun was not up.

She had a very birthday kind of feeling.

Her mother gave her a new school dress, and her father gave her a box of colored pencils. She tried on the dress, did two drawings with the pencils, and it was still just time for breakfast.

Sophie's stomach was too full of butterflies to have room for food.

"You must eat something," said her mother.

Then Sophie saw that it was her favorite, sticky coconut wrapped in banana leaves like tiny presents, and she was hungry after all.

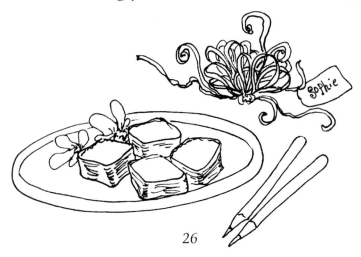

But when she had
finished, it was still a long,
long time until tea with
Ann-Marie.

"Could we go somewhere?" Sophie asked.

"Of course we can, if it is not too far," said her mother.

"And if it doesn't cost too much," said her father.

"We can walk there," said Sophie, "and it's free."

She told them where she wanted to go.

"A pet shop!" said her mother. "We can't have a pet here, Sophie."

"You know that would be impossible," said her father. "I'd start sneezing."

"And not with the twins so little," added her mother.

"I'd just like to look," said Sophie.

# Chapter 4

Sophie could not believe that they were really going.

They scrubbed the twins' hands and faces and dressed them in matching stripes; her mother combed her hair and her father locked the door. The elevator was broken again, so they *bump-thump-bumped* the twins' carriage down all the stairs to the bottom of the building.

They crossed the road at the lights, walked through the wide, green park, and . . .

. . . finally they were at *The Noahs' Ark.*
The ship was even bigger and brighter
and more beautiful than it had been from
Sophie's window.

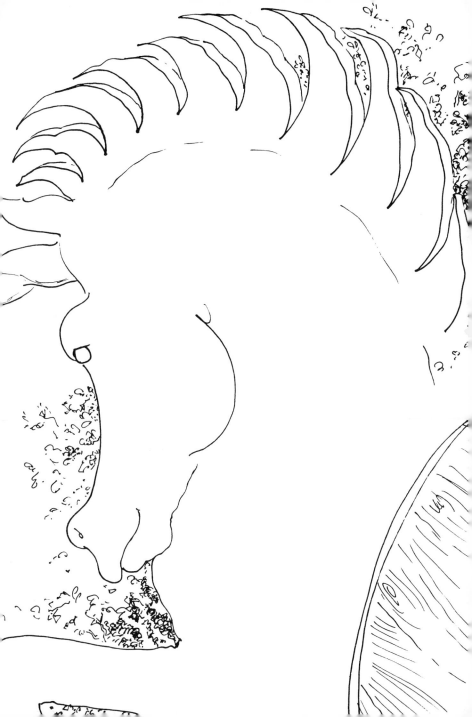

The long ramp up to the deck was like a ship's gangplank except that it was lined with pots of red geraniums and yellow daisies.

Mrs. Noah was watering the flowers.

Mrs. Noah was short and plump, with lively hands and small dark eyes that twinkled with a secret fire from somewhere deep inside her.

At the top of the ramp was a big wooden door with a large brass knocker in the shape of a dolphin.

Mr. Noah was polishing the dolphin.

Mr. Noah was tall and thin and a little stooped, with gentle hands and very clear, very blue eyes.

Sophie stood with one foot on the bottom of the ramp. She looked up and saw Mrs. Noah, Mr. Noah, the ship, and over them all the huge glass sails stretching to the sky. Little rays of morning sun, caught in the glass sails, bounced back in shattered colors like light through a prism.

"Oh," said Sophie. Just "oh."

Mrs. Noah and Mr. Noah stopped their watering and their polishing and stood together at the top of the ramp and looked back at Sophie.

"Good morning," said Mrs. Noah. "You're our very first visitors today."

"We're just looking!" said Sophie's mother.

"We don't want a pet!" said Sophie's father.

"You can look as much as you like," said Mr. Noah. "The animals enjoy seeing people."

Sophie did not say anything. She couldn't. She walked up the ramp and stood between Mr. and Mrs. Noah and looked all around. Mr. and Mrs. Noah looked at each other over Sophie's head and began to smile.

She saw cockatoos and canaries, parrots and budgies and tiny finches, and a peacock fanning his tail.

She saw fat black ponies and prancing gray ones, woolly lambs and dainty goats, and soft brown donkeys with a dark cross down their backs.

She saw big dogs and little dogs, dogs with shaggy hair and smooth hair, dogs with long tails and wagging tails and ears that trailed on the ground.

She saw black cats and tabby cats and tiny tumbling kittens, round silky-haired cats and cats with clear blue eyes.

She saw twitchy-eared rabbits and mop-haired guinea pigs, yellow quacking ducklings and fluffy clucking chicks.

She saw wrinkled old tortoises and tiny baby turtles, goldfish and angel-fish and fish with bright blue stripes.

And far down below she saw smooth and shining, coiling, twisting snakes.

"Oh," said Sophie. Just "oh."

Mr. and Mrs. Noah looked at each other over her head and smiled.

"Do you want to go for a walk?" they asked.

So Sophie, her mother and father, and the twins followed Mr. and Mrs. Noah all over the ship. Upstairs and downstairs, through the cabin and under the sails, to every corner of the seven decks.

When Sophie's father began to sneeze, Mr. Noah gave him a box of tissues and took him back to the office. There were no animals in the office, and after he had spent an hour looking at computers, cash registers,

and columns of numbers, Sophie's father began to feel better again.

And when Sophie's mother and the twins were tired, they sat in deck chairs in the sun, while Mrs. Noah bounced the twins on her lap and talked about babies and cities and being far away from home.

It had been a long time since Sophie's mother had spoken to anyone except Sophie and her father and the twins. But after a while she began to talk, and then smile and even laugh with Mrs. Noah.

# Chapter 5

**S**ophie went on visiting the animals. Her eyes and fingers were greedy with seeing and touching, and happiness was popping out all over her like chicken pox. But finally, "Sophie," said her mother, "it's time to go."

"We've been here for hours," said her father.

"Oh," said Sophie. But this time it was not a happy "oh," and when Mr. and Mrs. Noah looked at each other over her head they did not smile.

"It's her birthday," explained Sophie's mother. "Her friend is coming for tea."

"Which birthday?" asked Mrs. Noah.

"Seventh," said Sophie.

"My favorite number," said Mrs. Noah.

"Quite old, really," said Mr. Noah.

"Do you think," began Mrs. Noah, "that now she's seven . . ."

". . . she could come to see us again?" finished Mr. Noah.

"We could meet her at the crossing . . ."

". . . and make sure she doesn't get lost."

Sophie's mother and father thought about it.

"She won't be any trouble?" they asked.

"She'd be a great help," said Mrs. Noah.

"Well—since she's seven—," said her mother.

"Could I come next Saturday?" asked Sophie.

"We'll meet you at the crossing at eight," said Mr. Noah.

# Chapter 6

All that next week Sophie waited for it to be Saturday again. Now that she had seen *The Noahs' Ark*, it was even better than she had thought it would be. When the other children talked about what they were going to do and who they would see on the weekend, happiness bubbled up inside her and she thought about where *she* would go and who *she* would see.

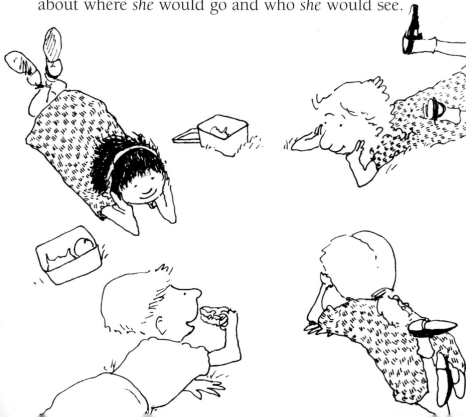

Every morning she sat at the window to eat her breakfast and stared across the park at the great white sails. She wanted it to be the weekend so badly, but was so afraid the Noahs would forget, or her parents would change their minds, that she could hardly swallow her fruit and cereal.

But on Saturday morning, when her hair was combed, her face was washed, and she was all dressed, her father just said, "We really can't have a pet, Sophie."

"I know," said Sophie, "but I like to see them."

"Would you like me to cross the road with you?" her mother asked.

"No," said Sophie. "I can do it myself."

"I'll watch from the window," said her mother.

So Sophie went all the way down the stairs and out the door and down to the lights. Waiting for her at the other side of the crossing were Mr. and Mrs. Noah and three dogs on leashes.

"We thought you wouldn't mind . . ." said Mrs. Noah.

". . . helping walk the dogs," said Mr. Noah.

Sophie didn't say anything. She took one of the leashes, waved to the window where her mother was watching, and walked across the park with Mr. Noah, tall and smiling, on one side and Mrs. Noah, small and twinkling, on the other and the three dogs running ahead on their leashes.

# Chapter 7

They walked up the gangplank with the geraniums and daisies in pots, and opened the door with the big brass dolphin. They took the dogs back to the dog deck, took off their leashes, and told them what good dogs they were.

"We haven't fed the birds yet," said Mr. Noah.

"Would you like to help?" asked Mrs. Noah.

Sophie was so happy that she thought she might burst.

"Where do you put the grain?"

"In your hands," said Mrs. Noah.

"So they'll come to you," added Mr. Noah.

"Because a pet must be a friend . . ."

". . . and some of them need a little help to learn how."

So Sophie stood very quietly inside the sails, and the birds swooped down to meet her. Some landed on her shoulders and her head while the quails and the peacock nestled around her feet. They cheeped and squawked and ate from her hands until all the grain was gone.

When they flew off, one of the parrots stayed on her shoulder.

"Sinbad," said Mr. Noah, "has a problem."

"He used to belong to a sailor and he says such terribly naughty things . . ."

". . . that he can't live with anyone else."

So Sophie sat down with Sinbad and taught him to sing "Polly Put the Kettle On" and "Frère Jacques." He sang them right through and then sang a very rude song in English and another in Spanish that sounded as if it would be even ruder if she could understand the words.

"Never mind," said Mr. Noah. "Maybe you could try some other songs next week."

"And if he learns enough," said Mrs. Noah, "maybe no one will notice the naughty ones."

52

At lunchtime Mrs. Noah made a picnic. She
carried the picnic basket out to the park, while
Sophie led a brown goat and Mr. Noah
led a white lamb. The lamb and the
goat cropped the grass while Sophie
and the Noahs ate their
picnic lunch.

# Chapter 8

When they went back to the ark, Mrs. Noah gave Sophie a ball of wool and a kitten who had never learned to play. Sophie dangled the wool until the kitten pounced, and wiggled it until the kitten jumped again. It patted at the wool and leaped into the air and turned somersaults.

When it was too tired to play anymore it curled up in her lap and purred. Sophie stroked it gently as it went to sleep, and the warmth of the kitten flowed up from her fingers and right through her body like sunshine.

A boy came with his mother and father, and saw the kitten sleeping in the wool on Sophie's lap.

"That's the one I want!" the boy said.

"Is it for sale?" his mother asked.

"How much is it?" asked his father.

Mr. and Mrs. Noah looked at each other over Sophie's head. They did not smile.

"It's for sale," they said.

The boy took the kitten. He was too excited to speak. Sophie didn't want to say anything either.

"I think he'll love it," Mrs. Noah said gently. "The kitten will be happy there."

"Come up on the dog deck, Sophie," said Mr. Noah. "There's a puppy who needs a run."

The puppy was fat and bouncy. Sophie taught it to chase a ball and play tug-of-war with a rag. Finally, the puppy tugged so hard that the rag flew out of Sophie's hands. She tumbled over backward with the puppy on top, and they rolled across the deck in a bundle of giggles and licks and scrabbling furry paws.

A tall lady stopped to watch them.

"That dog needs more exercise!" she said, and then laughed. "So do I. Is he for sale?"

Sophie got up. She stood very straight and looked back at the lady.

58

"Yes," she said.

Mr. and Mrs. Noah smiled.

Sophie picked up the puppy. He was squirmy and licky, but she hugged him in a last secret cuddle before she handed him to the lady. He licked the lady's nose and she laughed again.

"Where do I pay?" the lady asked.

Sophie went to the office, where Mrs. Noah showed her how to use the cash register. Then Sophie took the lady's money and sold her a collar and leash, a brush, and a ball.

When the puppy left, Sophie sat on Mrs. Noah's lap for a little while. She felt warm and safe. Saying good-bye to the kitten and the puppy didn't seem as bad as it had at first.

"Anyone," said Mrs. Noah, "can buy a pet. But you are making friends, and nobody can buy a friend."

"You see," said Mr. Noah, "sometimes when you can't have something that you want very badly, you find something else instead."

# Chapter 9

At five-thirty Mr. Noah hung the CLOSED sign on the dolphin knocker. Then he and Sophie and Mrs. Noah went upstairs and downstairs to every basket and kennel and pen and coop. They said good night to all the animals and checked that they were fed and happy for the night.

They had visited six of the seven decks, and Sophie knew it would soon be time to go. She wondered if the Noahs were going to walk her home across the park, but she didn't know how to ask. She wanted to say, "Can I really come again?" but the words froze and wouldn't come out.

She held on tightly to Mr. and Mrs. Noah's hands and wished the night would never come.

"This has been a crammed-full day," said Mrs. Noah. "And it's ended too soon!"

A warm wiggle slid through Sophie, melting the edges of the icy questions.

Sophie looked up and saw they were on the last deck of all—the pony deck. It smelled of sweet fresh hay, donkeys, and ponies.

The animals lifted their noses from thoughtful chewing, whickering softly. They looked lazy and sleepy. All except four white ponies who pranced around their stalls when the Noahs spoke to them, pricking up their ears and flicking long forelocks out of their eyes.

"They haven't been out today," said Mr. Noah.

"So if you don't mind . . ."

". . . we'll drive you home in the pony carriage."

Sophie had lived in the city all her life. She had ridden in cars and buses and trains, but she had never been inside a pony carriage.

"I was given this one for my seventh birthday," said Mrs. Noah. "My grandmother taught me to drive it."

"And with all these ponies," said Mr. Noah, "it seems a waste to have a car."

The carriage was red, and had bouncy springs, black painted wheels, and a high, padded seat. Sophie sat between Mr. and Mrs. Noah.

The ponies' hooves made neat round clopping sounds as they trotted down the gangplank and along the wide paths of the park. They stopped at the lights in front of Sophie's big apartment building.

"Maybe tomorrow you could learn to drive," said Mr. Noah.

"If you still want to come and see us again," Mrs. Noah said quickly, before the words froze and wouldn't come out.

# Chapter 10

On Sunday morning, Sophie got ready to visit the ark again.

"The Noahs are very busy people," her father said. "They can't come to meet you every day."

Sophie's insides twisted and sank down to her shoelaces. Her throat burned and her eyes stung. The sun disappeared and her world turned black.

"So, if you're careful," her mother said, "I'll watch from the window, and you can make your way by yourself."

"Take the path straight through the park," her father said. "And don't talk to strangers."

The sun came out and her world was splashed with color. Sophie kissed her mother and hugged her father and began to dance. The twins laughed and she swung them dizzily till they all fell down.

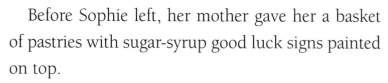

Before Sophie left, her mother gave her a basket of pastries with sugar-syrup good luck signs painted on top.

"I haven't made these cakes for a long time," she said, "but I think the Noahs would like them."

Sophie took the basket. She caught the elevator down and carefully crossed the road at the lights. She waved up at the window that was her home.

Then she ran down the path, all the way to *The Noahs' Ark*. Sophie knew it would be another crammed-full day, and she didn't want to waste any of it.

Every weekend after that, and on school holidays and sometimes after school, Sophie visited the ark.

She learned to help on all the different decks. Sometimes she mucked out the goats' stable and sometimes she filled the pond for the ducklings and sometimes, when she felt brave, she fed the snakes.

She helped Mrs. Noah water the flower pots and Mr. Noah polish the brass dolphin.

She picked grass for the guinea pigs, played ball with the dogs, and rode the ponies.

But what she liked best of all was making friends with the animals till they had homes of their own—and helping children choose pets that they would love.

When Sophie felt sad she remembered what the Noahs had said and, when she walked through the park, she knew they were right. The tall lady and the fat dog often ran down the path with her, and the boy with the kitten drew her a picture of the cat in its basket.

All through the park children with their pets smiled and waved when they saw her.

"It's Sophie!" they'd say. "From *The Noahs' Ark!*"

Sometimes she invited Ann-Marie to come with her to *The Noahs' Ark,* and sometimes she took the twins. Sometimes her father came to help Mr. Noah in his office, and her mother came occasionally when she had cooked something special and shared it with the Noahs.

But when Sophie visited by herself, that was the most special of all.

Before she went home Sophie and the Noahs always sat down together and had tea and the special cakes that Mrs. Noah baked for Saturdays, and they talked. Mrs. Noah taught her songs that she had sung when she was a girl, and Mr. Noah told her stories about when he was a boy.

# Chapter 11

One day Sophie told Mr. and Mrs. Noah about the three wishes she used to make.

"We had a wish that never came true," Mrs. Noah said, but her dark eyes twinkled and she did not sound sad. "We wished for children."

"And when we were too old for children," said Mr. Noah, "we wished for grandchildren. But we knew that was impossible."

And his blue eyes twinkled, too.

"I knew that the pet and the cousins were impossible," said Sophie. "But I didn't really care if it was cousins. I wanted an aunt or an uncle or . . ."

"Someone special to love you," said Mrs. Noah.

"Grandparents," said Sophie.

She held Mr. Noah's hand in her left hand, Mrs. Noah's in her right, and Mr. and Mrs. Noah looked at each other over Sophie's head and smiled as if they would never stop.

"Who says," said Mr. Noah, "that impossible wishes
can't come true?"